**For my Mamasaurus and Papasaurus —S. L.**

Library of Congress Cataloging-in-Publication Data available.

ISBN 978-1-4521-4425-2

Manufactured in China.

Design by Sara Gillingham Studio.
Typeset in Block Berthold and Paperback.
The illustrations in this book were rendered in brush pen and Photoshop.

10 9 8 7 6 5 4 3 2 1

Chronicle Books LLC
680 Second Street
San Francisco, California 94107

Chronicle Books—we see things differently.
Become part of our community at www.chroniclekids.com.

# PAPA SAURUS

**Stephan Lomp**

chronicle books · san francisco

Babysaurus lived in a wild jungle with his Papasaurus.

They loved to play hide-and-seek.

One day, it was Papasaurus's turn to hide.

"10,
9,
8 . . ."

When Babysaurus
finished counting,
he did not see his
Papasaurus anywhere.

But Babysaurus did see Stego.

"Have you seen my papa?"
Babysaurus asked.

"Does his back have spikes like
my papa's?" asked Stego.

"No, he has a round back with a long tail that I can slide down," Babysaurus answered.

"Then, sorry, no, I have not seen him," replied Stego.

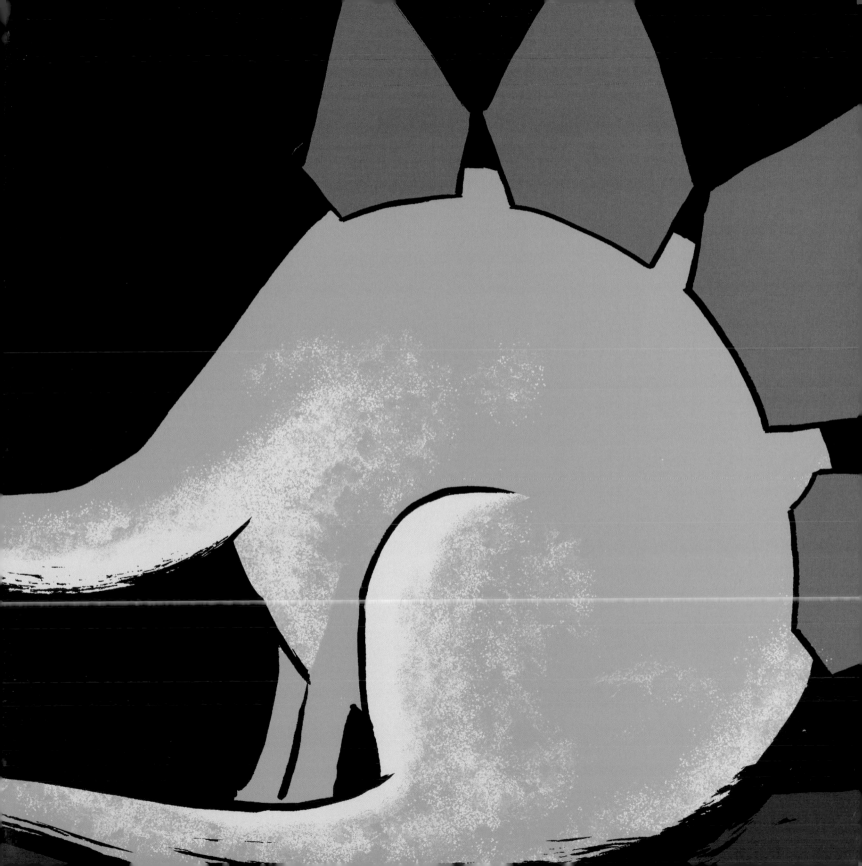

Babysaurus wandered through
the leafy jungle until he heard a
LOUD thumping sound.

"Excuse me!" he yelled over the noise.
"Have you seen my papa?"

"Can he knock down trees with his tail to gather fruits and leaves for dinner?" asked Anky.

"No," answered Babysaurus.
"He uses his long neck to
reach the tastiest leaves in
the tallest treetops."

"Then, no, I haven't seen him," said Anky.

Next Babysaurus saw
Mosa swimming in the sea.

"Have you seen my papa?"
Babysaurus called out.

"Does he have fins so he can
dive deep down into the water
like my papa?" asked Mosa.

"No," answered Babysaurus.
"But he has long legs that can
walk all the way across the jungle.
They are so long that I can stand
underneath him and be protected
from rain or sun."

"Oh!" said Mosa. "No,
I have not seen him."
Then she swam away.

Soon, Babysaurus saw Velo.
"Hey!" Babysaurus called out.
"Have you seen my papa?"

"Does he have sharp claws to fight like my papa?" asked Velo.

"No, he never fights," answered Babysaurus.
"Sorry, I have not seen him," said Velo.

Suddenly Babysaurus
saw something move
in the tall grass.

It was Edmont.

"Excuse me, have you seen my papa?" Babysaurus asked. "We are playing hide-and-seek."

"Does he hide in the grass sometimes like my papa?" asked Edmont.

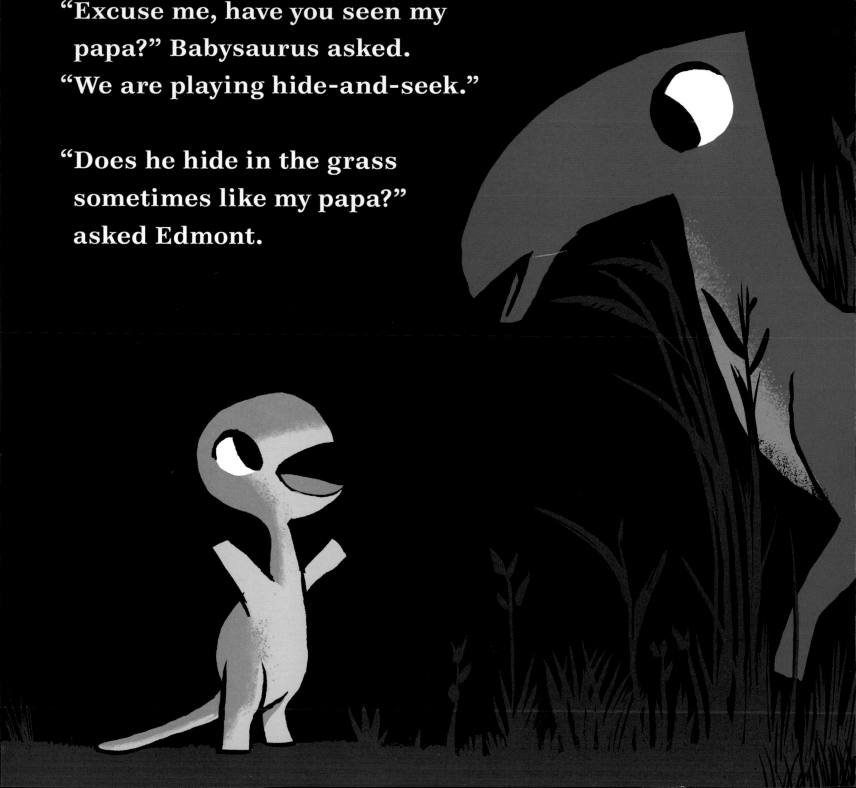

"It would be hard for him to hide in the grass. He is very big. The biggest there is!" Babysaurus exclaimed proudly.

"Then he should be easy to find!" replied Edmont.

Babysaurus stopped to think.
"Where could my papa be?"
he wondered.

Suddenly . . .

It was his papa! "There you are!" exclaimed Babysaurus. "I was searching all over for you!"

"You are a very good seeker," said
his papa, giving Babysaurus a kiss.
"Next time, you hide and I'll seek."

"Hooray!" cheered Babysaurus.

"You are the best Papasaurus in the whole jungle!"